Mommy Isn't Perfect

Samantha Powell

Mommy Isn't Perfect
Copyright @ 2022 by Samantha Powell

Preface

This book is for the young girl that wishes her mommy would have or could have told her more about how to operate as a young lady in this world. It includes key things that could save her from numerous mistakes if she were only taught how to avoid them. This book is meant to guide her with key mommy advice and tips on how to make it through middle school, high school, and young adulthood.

This book was written with my daughters and young girls around the world in mind. I am a mother of five beautiful girls—three of which came from my womb and two beautiful bonus daughters. The reality is that tomorrow is not promised for anyone, so I am choosing to write down everything I possibly can now while I am still of sound mind so that my girls for as well as those who aren't can get some authentic mommy advice while I'm still here to share.

Take a page out of Mommy Sam's book and learn from my mistakes so that you can avoid them or spot them a mile away. No more wishing you knew more. Some key fundamentals are right at your fingertips.

Contents

Part One

Quick Fundamentals

Chapter 1

"Who Runs the World"? (Girls)

Hello, lovely, I want to start by saying that you are unapologetically, perfectly made. You are effortlessly beautiful when you allow your true self to shine and your voice to be heard. It is because of the way you were designed that the world can continue in its existence. Understand that you are an intricate piece to this world, and do not allow anyone to convince you otherwise.

You Were Flawlessly Made

Your mother, with the help of the Divine, brought you into this world. She carried you in her womb, and whether you have thought of this or not, that was a display of love in itself. She shared her body with you (or had someone else she trusted to carry you) in order for you to have life. Either way it was a woman who had to do it! That takes a tremendous amount of strength and courage. So no matter the circumstances between you and her, ALWAYS be grateful for that.

I start by saying this so you can understand that you were born into this world by strength and courage and therefore strength and courage is your birthright. You are a powerful being, and even when you feel weaker than your true self, hone into the strength that is naturally within you.

There is a great strength in feminine energy, so embrace it and never let it be deteriorated by the world around you.

No matter the circumstances of how you were conceived, you are here for a powerful purpose. I am certain of this simply because you have chosen to open up this book and learn more about how to be the best version of yourself as a young lady and not make the same mistakes others have, and that is truly ingenious!

Mommy Tip

I want you to understand the power you hold within you *because* of the abundance of feminine energy you possess. You were created and held by a woman in her womb, and you were born into this world as such. If you can find a way to channel into that feminine energy alone, you can change the world in profound ways. There will be times when you forget the strength you have, but always try to remember what I am telling you now. You were created to make this world a better place, and that is solely because you are who you were born to be. The only one that can stop you from conquering anything in this world is you. Do not let the world alter your feminine energy or attributes. You are flawless in your natural state, and do not *ever* let anyone or even yourself convince you otherwise.

Chapter 2

Cleanliness Is Next to Godliness

Your body is your temple. You only get one, so keep it in top-notch shape. Let's start from the top.

Your Mouth:

Morning breath is a real phenomenon, and everyone has it, but the key is to eliminate it before you even breathe in someone else's direction. It's called common courtesy.

Mommy Tip:

Your mouth holds a tremendous amount of bacteria from the foods and drinks you consume. If you allow that food to sit in your mouth overnight, it practically eats away at your gums and the enamel of your teeth. What was once white (teeth) turns yellow, and what was once pink (gums) turns brown! Yuck! Keep that million-dollar smile, baby. It can make you tons of money one day!

Mommy Tip

Brush at minimum twice a day, once at night and once in the morning. If your teeth are already yellow, brush, brush, brush, and you can more than likely reverse it back to white at this young age. If your gums are brown, use a soft toothbrush and brush your gums and watch your gums go from brown to pink again! Woo-hoo, back to that million-dollar smile!

Your Armpits

Always check your armpits (in private, of course) because if you can smell it, more than likely someone else can too. This is one of those odors you shouldn't have as a young lady, at least for long.

Mommy Tip

If you need to freshen up those armpits, grab a wet towel (or napkin) and some feminine soap. Scrub away that funk and then rinse and dry. Once you are done, apply deodorant. Voilà, fresh as new! No excuse for downright disrespectful armpits.

Your Lady Parts and Bottom

Let's start with the basics: wiping. This may be the moment in this book where you are like, "Really?" But, yes, *really*!

Always wipe from front to back and never the opposite. You do not want the bacteria from your bottom to enter into your lady parts. This can cause a bacterial infection, which is extremely uncomfortable. Using a wipe is great when you have finished disposing the waste from your body out of your bottom.

Mommy Tip

The trick of disposing of your sanitary napkins (pads) is as follows:

- *Always* wrap it! Get some tissue or a napkin and wrap your sanitary napkin so no red residue can be seen and to mask odor.
- Never flush your sanitary napkin down the toilet.
- Be a sweetie and wipe the seatie.
- Pooping is natural—poop and then spray away. (People will stop laughing at it when they mature.)

Mommy Tip

- If aunt flow has come to visit this month, always use a feminine wipe to freshen up when you go to the restroom, and ALWAYS apply a fresh pad.
- If you are wearing a pad, it's best to wear fitted panties. You do not want air to hit your pad because it can release an odor. Fitted panties have the ability to prevent that.

- Also, NEVER wear white or a light color on your cycle.
- Keep extra panties and clothes in your locker or backpack. Accidents do happen.

Your Fingers and Toes

Keep your nails and toes free from dirt!

<u>Fact</u>: your fingernails tend to be dirtier than your bottom. Let that resonate. *Do not* bite your nails or suck your thumb.

If possible, keep those toes polished with a nice clear coat and nicely groomed. Colored polish is a plus but not necessary. Remember, in almost all cases natural is the way to go.

General Body

Rinse, scrub, repeat! Rinse, scrub, repeat! Rinse, scrub, repeat! Bathe, child, bathe, at minimum every night before bed. This way you can clean away the residue from the day you just conquered. Also, create a sleep routine. Your mind and body like consistency.

Check Out Momma Sam's Favorite Night Bathing Routine

Take a warm bath with the perfect light setting for that moment. Get some melatonin body scrub and bubble bath. Scrub away all your dead skin and allow that melatonin to soak in. By the way, melatonin is a hormone your body naturally produces in response to darkness. It ultimately helps you relax. There are now supplements or products that promote a healthy night's sleep.

Here is the flat-out truth. Your hygiene has the ability to reflect how you love and take care of yourself. Before you truly can love anyone else, you have to love yourself. Show everyone the love you are capable of giving by how you love and take care of yourself!

Mommy Pro Tip

Keep a hygiene bag in your backpack and/or purse. Equip it with your young lady sanitary napkins so that if you ever need to go take care of yourself during that time of the month or in general, you have everything you need

Hygiene bag list (making this bag stylish helps with self-esteem when you are on your cycle).

- Pads
- Feminine wipes
- Mouthwash
- Floss
- Deodorant
- Feminine soap
- Tissue
- Sanitizer
- Spray

Chapter 3

Culture Shock

At one point in time, everyone was not deemed to be equal, and some were considered to be less than. And then there was a time when everyone was said to be separate but equal. During both of those times, a lot of culture, as well as dignity, was lost for numerous generations before you.

Today cultures have blended in so many ways that it has compounded into the world you see today. And in modern culture, there are a lot of followers and not enough leaders. Being a part of social media in some form has become the new norm. With this new reality comes the fact that you are massively influenced by social media, and that affects the way you think about yourself and the world.

It is easy to compare yourself to those around you and on social media, but the sad truth is that the way those people portray themselves on social media may not be a true depiction of them in real life. I want you to think of it like this: a picture is worth a thousand words, but you determine the message. Basically, if someone wants you to see happiness, they will portray that in the picture or video. If someone wants you to believe they have money, they will portray that message. If someone wants you to buy their new product, they will portray a message that makes you believe that you need what they have in order to become or look like them. That is the sad truth, and at the end of the day, it is all a sales tactic to make you believe whatever they want you to believe. But here is what you must do in response: do not fall for the hype or follow the crowd, do not be envious, and most importantly, do not adjust anything about your unique self to be like someone else and as do many others in this world. As long as you stay your true authentic self, the world will succumb and help you shine one way or another. It will have no choice. Eleanor

Roosevelt once said, "Comparison is the thief of joy." So choose to be joyful, gorgeous. You will always see the world not how it is but the way that you are. Culture can not define you. Only you can do that!

Mommy Tip

With no judgment in my heart, I ask this of you, sweet girl. If you do consider going the route of entertainment of any kind, you first do your research on how being an influencer has impacted people's mental health, good and bad, as well as their fulfillment of life.

Chapter 4

Give Yourself Some Grace

There will be many times in your life when you will make a mistake. Sometimes you will even wonder to yourself how you allowed yourself to do such a "stupid" thing. But know that a mistake is never stupid, because it can teach you a key lesson that makes you grow or shrink. How you respond to that lesson with either growing or shrinking is up to you. Shrinking looks something like this: you make a mistake and blame others and do not take responsibility for your actions. You may also choose to become negative-minded and change something about your authentic self to appease others. You may even ridicule or be hard on yourself. Whereas giving yourself some grace looks like this: you make a mistake, and you take responsibility for your actions. You learn from that mistake, and you never try to intentionally make that mistake again. You took away the key lesson from that mistake, and you grew from it. You became a better person because of it. That is important to understand: every heartache, pain, or mistake can help you grow. So never see a mistake as stupid. Look at it as an opportunity to grow and learn from it. There may even be times when you fall short. You may have had an assignment due, but you accidentally left it at home, and now you will lose credit, or maybe you forgot to do your chores, and now you can't go to your friend's house. Whatever the case may be, grow and do not shrink.

Mommy Tip

When you have disappointed yourself or others, give yourself some grace. You have not become the person you are today overnight. Sometimes change takes time, and we all make mistakes. There is absolutely no reason to be so hard on yourself that you feel less than. Pick your head up and digest the mistake or circumstance, feel it, learn from it, and then shake it off. At the end of the day, you have to keep pressing forward no matter what.

Part Two

A Whole New World

Chapter 5

Stranger Things

Right around the time you hit middle school, or shortly after, your body will start showing noticeable changes. Your once child-like figure will start expanding in different ways to become more "ladylike." Your emotions will seem to become more heightened, and your attraction to boys might seem to grow out of nowhere. This is called puberty. Although a lot of people believe that this begins once "aunt flow" pays her first visit, it can actually happen quite some time before that. Regardless, this is the point when everything and everyone around you may start to look a little different. You may become interested in trying new things that you were not interested in before. Here is a great example: around this time, many kids seem to desire to have their "first kiss." This desire comes around this time usually because the body is producing new hormones that make you attracted to other people more than they did in the past. It makes you want to become more interactive with others. Here is the key: it is important to remember during this time to try not to act on impulses caused by your body changing the way that it is.

When I was in the sixth grade, out of nowhere, I started to need a bra more than usual. I had to progress out of the training bra stage because my body was growing at the rate that it was. I was getting far more attention from boys, but truthfully, not in the most respectful way all the time. This is very common for most girls around this age, but there is a way to handle it.

Mommy Tip

Young boys around this time are extremely immature. They may try to touch you inappropriately by touching your bosom or your bottom. If by chance they do attempt and possibly even succeed, you must stand your ground to make sure they understand they can never do that again. You are a young queen and should be treated with the utmost respect and decency. I suggest responding in the following manner with authority: "This is NOT your body. DO NOT touch it like it is!"

Always stay classy. Keep yourself covered, but do not be ashamed of the new body you are in. There is a way to show off your new body without showing all of your skin. Figure out the most ladylike way to do that so you demand respect. But the only person's attention you should ever crave is your own. Self-love is the best love.

Chapter 6

Middle School Blues

At the beginning of middle school, I had two close friends. We were pretty much always together, and for the most part, everyone knew who we were around the school. Out of the three of us, you had one that was the most popular, one that followed right behind her, and then me, coming in third on the popularity chart.

During this point in my life, I was very quiet, and my grades were always superb, so I was considered the "smarter" and "quieter" one out of the group. In my defense, I was not a quiet person at all, just very observant. I was great at paying attention to detail and how people acted one way around one person and another way around someone else.

I couldn't understand why people seemed to change their character around certain people. This was uncool to me, and I felt like I could never become one of those people... until I was. Yes, I ended up changing myself. Let's dive into how exactly.

As I mentioned, I used to be quiet, and truthfully, I was kind of a pushover as well at times only because people took my quietness for weakness. They seemed to bully me for answers to homework and sometimes even tests. Before middle school, I remember thinking to myself that I was a very sweet and smart girl, but after getting there, I wanted to be different so people did not take advantage of me. Sadly, that is exactly what I did.

I remember people telling me that I smiled too much, so I stopped smiling like I used to. Kids would call me a nerd, so I stopped portraying myself as such in front of them. (I still kept good grades.) People said that I was too quiet, so I started speaking out more. At the end of the day, I ended up doing exactly what I said I couldn't understand earlier, and that was change my character.

This is a BIG no-no. Stand firm in who you are. If someone says you are too smart, tell them to catch up. If someone says you are too quiet, tell them, "You are too loud." If someone tells you that you are weird, ask them, "Why are you concerned about me?" These people will stop messing with you as soon as they realize they cannot change the way you are feeling about yourself. Bullies like to see a reaction, so never give them a reaction. Instead give them a reality check.

Mommy Tip

There is a way to stand up for yourself without having to change yourself. Remain that sweet and smart girl. Those same people that laugh and try to take advantage of your quietness and smartness now will like and want to be around you when you are older. Why? Because you will grow up to be the smart woman that has her life together while those people who once treated you wrong will still be trying to find their way. Do not change your character at this point in your life due to bullying or pressure, because once you do, it will be hard to get back to who you used to be. This is what I can guarantee you: One day as an adult, when you look back on your life, you will want to be that same girl you once were before your middle school blues. Be sure to stand your ground when it comes to who you are, because you are naturally amazing and filled with greatness, and people like you make the world a more beautiful place. Be around people who fill you with joy and not sadness, so you can remain your true self.

Chapter 7

He Loves Me, He Loves Me Not

I had a crush in middle school, eighth grade to be exact, who turned out to be my "high school sweetheart" for most of my high school career. Surprisingly, he was a very popular guy, and everyone was very fond of him. On the other hand, I was still that not-so-popular girl. And because of that fact, no one seemed to be able to wrap their head around why I was the one he had chosen to be with. They started rumors that me giving away my innocence had to be the only way he would have chosen to be with me. This was not the case at all, actually, but people say what they want to believe, and I was their main target when it came to getting him for their own.

Once we were finally able to be at the same school together in tenth grade, it seemed like everything began unraveling. He became so popular that girls all around wanted to be his BFF, and that is exactly what they became. The more girl "friends" he had, the more insecure I became, and the more I started to pick fights with him because I no longer trusted him.

I felt like I was supposed to be the only girl in his world, and it seemed like I never was. This made me feel like I was not enough for him because he needed more girls around him than just me. I was stressed at a young age because of this relationship, but it taught me so much about myself. It laid the foundation of what love was supposed to feel and look like in my mind. This boy was my first love. To get him and keep him, I did things that I probably should not have. I felt the need to give up my innocence later on in our relationship in hopes of being able to keep him by my side. Sadly, that did not keep him. He eventually broke up with me to be with a girl that had supposedly been one of those BFFs. Although that relationship did not last more than two weeks, he broke me when he left me for someone else.

I remember feeling a pain so bad in my heart that I fell to my knees and could hardly breathe. I remember crying and having a panic attack for the first time in my life. I eventually yelled for my mom to come and rescue me from the panicked state I was in, and she did.

She asked me repeatedly what was wrong, but I could not calm down for the longest time. When I finally revealed to her what was causing me so much agony, these were her exact words: "Baby, do not ever let a boy get you this down again in your life. No boy is worth more than your sanity." She did not say anything more or anything less. Her words resonated within my soul and my heart, and I would never let a boy break me down to my knees ever again in my life.

Looking back now, I wish I would have kept my innocence and shared that special moment with my husband instead. Which is why I'm sharing this story with you. If there is ever someone who makes you feel insecure about *anything* about yourself, then they are not the right person for you. Learn what you can from them and move on. See, the best person for you will nurture your insecurities and make them seem like pure perfection because they truly are just that.

Mommy Tip

The first cut is the deepest, and it will hurt. It is okay to cry, to scream, and even to take some time for yourself, but whatever you do, do not shut yourself out to the ones around you that love you and bring you joy. The people that bring you joy are the very ones who can help you feel better during this time. Shutting people out is not the same as taking time to yourself. It is healthy for you to talk about the pain and truly digest why you are hurting the way you are . . . but the key is truly feeling. Only when you truly feel can you truly heal. If you try to brush this pain under the rug, it will subconsciously follow you the rest of your life and shape who you become. Do not let pain scold you, but mold you into someone greater. Always take note after every successful and failed relationship so you know what to look out for, whether good or bad, in the future. And, yes, relationships that did not work out can still be deemed successful!

Mommy Tough Love Tip

1. Accept! Accept that this relationship with your first love did not work out.

2. Feel! Feel the sadness that may come with the realization of the relationship ending.

3. Release! Let go of all that sorrow so you can move through the process of healing.

4. Recalibrate! Now that this love has run its course in your life for the season that it has, it is now time to focus on self love. This will help you get back to your joyful spirit and insightful self.

5. On to the next great love! As long as you stay in tune and take note of the good and bad of every relationship, your next love will be a greater love because you have calibrated yourself to receive even better whenever that time may come. Push the type of love in the world that you want from someone else, and you will get exactly that in return.

Chapter 8

Tornado Prom Night

By my prom night, I had been dating my boyfriend at the time for six months. I was eighteen, and I was a senior in high school. My mom was not as enthusiastic about prom as I wish she would have been, but she did buy me a nice purple and silk dress. I tried my best to make my hair as fancy as I could. I was even allowed to wear makeup for the first time, but I did have to do it myself. In my mind, this was already not going as planned because my mom wasn't snapping a million photos of me with the camera, I had to do my own hair and makeup, and I really did not feel as pretty as I would have liked to have felt at that very moment.

My boyfriend did not know how to drive at the time, so I ended up driving my big brother's black Avalanche truck. It was *huge*. I ended up picking up my prom date and not the other way around as I had seen on TV shows and movies. My prom date kept managing to step on my dress, which irritated me even more, and to top it off, prom ended early due to a tornado warning. EPIC FAIL prom night . . . at least that was my perspective at the time.

But looking back on prom night now, it was quite eventful. I may not have had a mother who was snapping tons of photos, but she was present in that moment with me as I got ready. I may have not had a makeup artist or a stylist, but at least I knew enough for the results to get me tons of compliments at prom. Although I did not get picked up for prom night, at least I had a brother that was kind enough to let me borrow his nice, fancy, detailed truck. Also, I had someone next to me who I really cared for at the time. It may not have been my ideal prom night, but it was my prom night story to tell one day. It is okay for this day not to go perfectly. Just be grateful and take notice of all the things that are coming together for you one way or another.

Mommy Tip

There is this notion going on that prom night is supposed to go absolutely perfect, but chances are that it will not go as exactly as planned, and that is okay. See, this is only one day of your entire life, and if it happens to be a "disaster," tomorrow can always be better. Get creative. Maybe you can have a dance party with your friends or family to have a redo of the prom night gone wrong. But on this night, remember to stay true to yourself and never do anything you truly do not want to. And for your heart's sake, do not feel pressured into not keeping your innocence. That is not what this night is about! This night is truly about being with your friends and getting dolled up and making good memories with those you care about the most. That is it!

Part Three

All Grown Up

Chapter 9

Girls Go to College to Get Smarter

Roadmap 101

I was always taught to have a plan A and a plan B just in case plan A somehow managed not to work out. So I took up the majors of nuclear engineering and radiological sciences and pre-med. My plan A was to be a doctor, while my plan B was to be a nuclear engineer. Unfortunately, after three years of continuous year-round school with some of the hardest majors in college, I started to become burnt out. My grades started plummeting because my classes were becoming harder for me to keep up with. I became overwhelmed, yet my parents kept pushing me to keep moving forward and just finish the degree. In my spirit I knew that I needed a break, and I ended up taking one. That break was everything I needed to recalibrate or rethink the path I was heading toward. It took me six years to return to college, but that was after the new business I had started and sold and even after I had my first child. I returned to college knowing *exactly* what it was that I truly wanted to do with my future, and that made the whole entire college experience different this time around. I did not feel any pressure to get through college because I knew without a doubt what I had come to do, and I did just that.

1st College Party

It was about six of us that got invited to our first college party freshman year by a senior. We were so excited about what the night would hold. We ended up dancing our hearts out and having a blast because we never left each other's side. Who we came with was who we partied with, and that was key to the night being a success. If you have a group of friends that are indulging in things like drinking, always always make sure that you or someone else is not drinking so there is a designated *safe* driver. You love your friends, so be the one to protect your friends.

Mommy Tip

Have an idea of where you are headed before you get there. There are so many paths you can take in college. Sometimes the many choices can become overwhelming. I suggest before you step foot on any college campus that you do your due diligence in researching the field you are considering. Create a research paper on the desired study and the paths it can lead you to. Find out about salary, work-life balance, and growth paths within the field that allow for you to keep progressing. Choose a path that brings out the fire and passion within you. Do not choose a path because of money or because someone else is "making you." This is your life, and you only have this time to do the things that bring you the utmost joy and promote the best version of you. Also, if you have to take a mental health break for your sanity, do not let anyone stop you. They will understand once you get to where you are truly going!

Mommy Pro Tip

Drinks

- If possible, always get a drink with a top on it.
- Keep a napkin over your drink.
- Never leave your drink unattended or attended by a stranger.

Your BFF

- Who you came with is *always* who you should leave with unless your safety is at risk. Keep an eye on each other at all times.

Alcohol and drugs

- Alcohol is a toxin to your body. It has not proven to be more healthy for you than it is bad. Your body does not know how to release these toxins, which lead to hangovers and impaired vision and thinking. Alcohol truly makes you less smart. Drugs and alcohol can have substances placed in them that can deteriorate your mind and the functions of your organs. If I had it my way, I would not want you to drink alcohol or do drugs ever in your life. But if you do take that road most traveled by, please do not forget my tips and the harm that you are doing to your beautiful self.

Chapter 10

Being My Own Boss

At twenty-three, I was a business owner of a nail, hair, and massage parlor known as The Ladies Parlor. It was an endeavor that my mother and I chose to take on together. I had a total of ten employees and no idea how to be a business owner. My mother, on the other hand, had over twenty years of experience under her belt. Therefore, I trusted that the business would be a success with her by my side helping me operate it. All I knew was that I wanted to be my own boss and that this had to work.

The first step to getting the business started was to find a location. Location is everything when it comes to the success of your business. For example, you do not want to put a nail, hair, and massage parlor behind a gas station where it is only visible when driving down that one particular street. This was my mistake #1. The two available spaces to rent were side by side, and both had empty spaces which could make the vision of my parlor come true. I was given the option to take both units, and I could knock open a wall that would connect them both. I ended up with 3,400-square-foot parlor. This was my mistake #2. When you are a new business, although your vision may be big and bold, it is important to outgrow your space rather than grow into your space. I started too big when I should have started with only one space vs. two. Unfortunately at the time, I could not see how to shrink my original vision, which led to the overhead bills of my parlor being too expensive monthly, which ultimately led to the demise of the business. We ended up selling the business and everything in it to another beautician for not even half the price we paid for it. I felt so defeated that I packed up my family and moved back to my hometown.

Mommy Tip

1. The best you can do is all that you can do. Although I felt defeated because my first business did not become as successful as I would have like, I still gained so much valuable experience. This, in turn, means I truly did not fail. Everything I learned from this first business I will take to the next, and the same will go for you if you keep persevering.

2. Being an entrepreneur is not an easy role. It takes tons of devotion and perseverance to keep pushing forward to obtain the results you truly want. In the beginning, those that are not entrepreneurs may not understand why you chose to go the "less stable" route. The route with no "guaranteed or steady" income exists, at least in the beginning. This is simply not the case. With proper goal setting and business planning, you can make a steady income and 3Xs more than the average person would working a nine to five. This is not for everyone as a career, but I do suggest that you attempt at least once

in your life to find a way to monetize what you are passionate about. It will do wonders for your mindset and future.

3. Buy equipment and other things for your business using business credit and not your personal credit. If the business plummets, that debt will not be carried on your personal credit. It will follow the business and not you.

Mommy Pro Tip

Family and business partnering may not always be the best route. There tends to be a lot more emotion involved when it comes to family. Sometimes these emotions can get in the way of the success of a business or even worse, cause friction between family members that did not exist prior to the business, so always weigh out your options thoroughly when starting a new business. Attempt fundraising prior to family handouts if at all possible.

Part Four

Just Keep Swimming

Chapter 11

No Pain, No Gain

You will face disappointments, setbacks, and heartaches in your life. We all do. This is how we are strengthened and reminded of the warriors that we truly are. When you feel as though you have failed at a goal or something was just out of your reach, understand that failure is the highway to success and getting knocked down is the price of ambition. As it has been said by one of the greats, "Get knocked down seven times and get back up eight." You have to learn to pivot and find the workaround in any circumstance that did not go as planned. One of my favorite coaches said, "Every time you see a wall, do not see it as a wall. See it as an opportunity." This is when you must be resilient and see how to optimize the circumstance.

> *"Turn your problems into projects because a problem is only a problem if you see it as one."*

> —R. Sharma

Mommy Tip

1. When you hear a no, it is just a yes in the making.

2. Be okay with being uncomfortable, so you can become comfortable.

3. Do not quit something you really love. Keep persisting, and over time, you will hit mastery.

4. All wounds heal, but first you must acknowledge that you are hurting.

5. One person hurting you doesn't assure that the next person will. You will be stronger for the next person, so do not fear.

6. Fear: Fear everything and run, or face everything and rise. Choose to rise!

7. If something does not work out, there is always something better for you.

8. "The only place where *success* comes before *work* is in the dictionary" (V. Lombardi). Meaning in order to have success, you must work. It will not just come to you.

9. If it looks like poop and smells like poop, then it is poop. Do not try to change what it already is.

10. No pain, no gain.

Chapter 12

The Woman You Are Becoming

Learn to focus on self-love rather than the love you receive from those around you. Self-love is truly the best love, and every time you do something good for yourself, more of your gold starts to see the light of day.

It is never too late to become the person you want to be. If you want to be a nicer person, become a nicer person. If you want better friends, surround yourself with better people. If you want to be the best athlete on the team, practice like no one else practices.

Whomever you choose to become, make sure you are staying true to yourself. At birth you were given stunning gifts and talents, and the world may have made you forget that. Once you start working on being better every day, you will start remembering who you truly are.

Mommy Tip

1. Do you remember what you wanted to be when you grew up? Think about why you wanted to do that job. That may not be what you want to be now, but there was something about that job that intrigued you, and maybe your future job should have that key thing.

2. Take care of yourself first so you can take better care of others.

3. If it does not bring you joy, get rid of or stop doing whatever it is. That is not considered quitting. That is being self-aware and in tune with your inner self.

4. Every day, strive to be a better version of yourself than yesterday.

5. You may have been dealt a different deck of cards than someone, but you still can

accomplish the same things. You just have to play a little bit smarter and harder. But no worries, you were made for this!

6. You only get this one chance at this life. Make it your best one!

7. Make time to exercise now, or you will be preparing to make time for your sickness in the future.

8. Start with making today great, because great days turn into great weeks, and great weeks turn into great months, and great months turn into great years, and great years turn into a great life.

9. Stretch *daily* so that your body does not get stiff!

10. Live and love life with NO EXCUSES!

Bonus

Purchasing Your First Home

In most states the minimum age to purchase a home is eighteen. As of 2022, you need the following at minimum to qualify for a home:

- A good credit score
- At least a 3 percent down payment of the purchase price of the home you are looking to buy
- At least 1.5% for closing costs, for good measure
- Two years' worth of tax returns in the same job field
- Check stubs
- Low debt-to-income ratio

Homebuying Process

1. Meet with a real estate agent.

2. Get preapproved by a mortgage lender. Being prequalified is not the same thing.

3. Search for homes.

4. Make an offer.

5. Contract negotiation.

6. The home status is pending until the closing date (or the date the home officially becomes yours.

7. Inspection and appraisal are completed on the property.

8. Closing—this the transfer of funds and ownership.

Mommy Tip

1. **Building Credit:** If at all possible, if your parents have good credit, ask them to put you on their credit as an authorized user so that you can have your credit built by their good habits. If this is not an option or the best option, then I suggest you get a secured credit card. You will have to put forth money first, but that will start the credit building process.

2. **Debt:** One of the worst mistakes I could have made as a new adult was trading in my car that had been paid off by my mom for a car that had a car note. DO NOT do this. I traded in an asset for debt.

3. **Savings Plan:** Start NOW! If you want that dream home in the future, then do what is difficult now so you can have what you desire in the future. Even if it is $20 a week. Start saving something!

4. **First-Time Homebuyer Programs:** You can usually search for programs in your area, but if you don't have any luck, your realtor should be able to assist you.